Killer Cure
by Aeriell Lawton
Copyright 2013 Orion Publishing House

Dedication

To "T",
Someone that I admire
and am honored
to be among her friends.

Chapter 1

Dr. Maggie Simmons was hunched over a microscope in the research and development lab of White Light pharmaceuticals. It was 2:45 AM, and she'd been staring at the microscope for so long that she was starting to get a migraine, and the edge of her vision was becoming blurry, but she had to know for sure. There was too much at stake not to be 100% certain. She scribbled some notes, rapidly on a legal pad that was on the table next to the microscope double checking and even triple checking the information and results of the tests that she had been running since 9:30 PM that evening. There was no mistaking it, this particular formula for the new drug White Light was producing would cause liver failure, kidney failure and possibly lead to cancer.

Her mind was racing frantically now. "There's no way we can let this out into the world. It would be like opening Pandora's box" she was pretty sure the results she was seeing in the microscope in the dark and graveyard quiet laboratory, where the real test results, and not the ones that were submitted to the FDA had been altered to show extremely promising results for the drug, which had been developed to help treat multiple sclerosis, also known as MS, which is a degenerative disease that affects the body's central nervous system and affects the brain's ability to communicate with the spinal cord and the rest of the body. The symptoms vary widely from patient to patient, but the most common symptoms include spasticity in the affected area such as the arms and legs. Hearing loss and inability to speak properly, a constant severe pain, and worst of all, it will eventually affect a person's ability to swallow. And although certain symptoms may come and go throughout the course of the disease others will be more permanent and severe depending on how far the disease has progressed. The individual suffering from the disease will eventually die due to the inability for the nerves to send the proper signals to the body that allow the lungs to function and even the heart to pump. It was a death that Maggie would not wish on her worst enemy.

The results that Maggie had screaming at her from a microscope and computer database, testified beyond a shadow of a doubt, that one in five individuals who took this medication that was supposed to be a miracle drug for the disease would develop horrendous complications that would cause them even more unnecessary pain and suffering on top of that provided by the disease itself. And although one in five people does not seem like a very high number when you multiply that by the number of people on the planet that were dealing with the disease and who had been waiting on pins and needles for this supposedly miracle drug to greatly improve their quality of life. The result could be catastrophic. There could be millions of people that would suffer and die needlessly.

All in the name of what profit she could not believe someone at a company with such an ethical reputation as that of White Light pharmaceuticals, would stoop to doctoring study results in order to make a profit it had to be slightly more complicated than that, it just had to be Maggie could not bring herself to believe otherwise she knew she had to report her findings to the FDA immediately. And because she did not know for certain who else at the company would be aware of this corruption. She had opened up her phone and was placing a call to Mark Callahan, a reporter friend who works for the Seattle Sun and was always interested in a good corporate conspiracy and corruption story. She bit her nails nervously as the phone began to ring. She began rocking back and forth on her heels causing her 5'6" frame to sway gently back and forth like a little in the wind the phone was on its fourth ring, and the voicemail message engaged with the beep "this is Mark Callahan. I am currently away from my desk, but if you leave your name and number. I will get back to you as soon as possible."

"Hello Mark. It's Maggie; I've got something you should see the avenging Angel has a broken sword. The drug doesn't work, well, I mean, it does. But it's got some horrible side effects. We've got to let people know; meet me for coffee tomorrow morning at 10 AM at the Blue Bean Café. And I will explain everything. Call me back as soon as you get this message. So I know you understand, because the drug goes online in two days." She ended the call dropped the phone into the right-hand pocket of her lab coat, scooped up her research, pulled her glasses from the top of her head, placing them in their rightful place on the bridge of her nose while simultaneously causing her bright red hair to fall haphazardly into her face. She brushed it away quickly and gave one last glance around her workstation.

To make absolutely sure she had not forgotten anything, and because she did not want anyone to realize what she had been doing, confident that she had all the evidence on her person she dashed toward the door out of the lab and bounded down the stairs two a time until she reached the front door in the main lobby at which point she almost dropped the load she was carrying, because she had to swipe her key card to unlock the door. She was so nervous and anxious. It took her three times before the door finally clicked open but when it did, she pushed it open violently and headed off down the street in the direction of her apartment, which was only six blocks away.

Chapter 2

Detective Ian Rite was placing his nicely broken in motorcycle jacket on the back of his chair at his desk while removing his helmet. He decided to ride his Triumph Bonneville in to work this morning to take advantage of the semi-decent weather, because although it was mildly chilly as the thermometer was only reaching about 51 this morning. He felt that the cold fresh air, would give him just what he needed to start his first day as a homicide detective on the right foot as he was on loan from the zombie squad. He had requested this particular tour of duty because he was beginning to feel that he might be on the ragged edge as being a member of the deep undercover squad takes a hefty toll on all of its officers, all the lies that must be kept straight bogeys worrying whether someone was becoming suspicious. Not being able to call friends and family on a regular basis was absolutely mentally exhausting. So after his last case with the zombies had successfully been closed he went to his commanding officer and asked for a transfer in hopes of saving his sanity.

Rite had joined the Seattle Police Department after being honorably discharged from the Marine Corps at the age of 25. Seattle, being his last duty station, he decided to stay because he fell in love with the majestic mountain scenery and easy access to any adventurous activity you could desire. He had enrolled in the police Academy, because he felt that the police force would be similar in structure and brotherhood to that of the Marine Corps. It was a job that would allow him to continue to serve the people. He had joined the zombie squad, because he still desired the action he had experienced as a Special Forces operator. He knew that the zombie squad got the most exciting assignments, and that it was also the fastest way to learn the gold shield of a Detective, which he had held for the last 15 years.

As he sat down in his chair he fingered the gold shield on his belt it felt strange to be wearing his credentials so openly, it kind of unnerved him actually as ordinarily they would be tucked away in a secret pocket and only brought on very special occasions. Having someone accidentally catch a glimpse of them usually meant serious trouble. Like his cover being blown. He felt himself, working his eyes around the room as though he was checking to see if anyone was going to make a move. He had to shake his head several times, and reminded himself that he was indeed a police officer, as were most of the individuals in the room. As he was absentmindedly adjusting the straps on the shoulder holster that contained his Beretta 9 mm, he was greeted by the sound of someone clearing their throat. He looked up from his task to see Capt. Magdalena Swift, peering down at him through the top half of the lenses of her stainless steel wireframe glasses that were perched on the tip of her nose, and her long black hair that was starting to gray slightly was tied up in a tight bun. All of this in combination with the black pants suit she was wearing and the folder she was holding in her hand made her look to Rite more like an overzealous librarian rather than the battle hardened veteran detective she was.

"Good morning Rite and how are we settling in?" She said with a half smile, and any time that was trying to be friendly and welcoming, but came across as something she was forced to do because of protocol. Rather than something she actually enjoyed "everything is fine, sir. Just making sure my workstation and equipment are shipshape and squared away." He said with a preprogrammed response. "That's very good. I've just been going over your paperwork here." She said gesturing with the file "and it seems you are, quite an officer. Lots of high-profile arrests bikers Mafia dons, and even a serial killer." She said, sounding only semi-impressed. "You should be an excellent addition to homicide." Well, I hope so, sir. I plan on giving you 110%, at all times." "I'm sure you will, but I didn't come over here just to exchange pleasantries. I wanted to introduce you to your partner.

This is Autumn Summers." She said, gesturing to a blond haired, brown eyed woman who appeared to Rite to be about 5'5" tall and very athletic and in her mid-30s, Autumn stepped forward and offered her hand to Rite who immediately noticed that she had a very firm commanding grip which to him directly signified that she had confidence, which is a necessity for any detective. "Nice to meet you, I look forward to working with you. I think I can learn a lot from you." She said with a wink and a half smile. "I feel the same I believe we can learn a lot from each other." Ian said with a smile. "Detective Summers will show you the ropes and help you find your feet as the detective. It might be a good idea if she was the lead detective on any case; the two of you should catch for the next few months just until you're comfortable, with only operating procedures, of course."

"That is absolutely fine with me", Rite said. "Good then I will leave the two of you to your business." Capt. Swift said, and then abruptly turned and walked back into her office. Rite and Summers felt comfortable with each other. Almost immediately as though they had been friends for a long time, but had never realized it until now they discussed all the necessary cop shop small-talk like their best and worst case how many years on the police force (she had 12) best place for takeout when on a surveillance detail all the necessary information that Rite would need to survive as a homicide detective in the department.

Rite was starting to wonder exactly what they would spend their day doing when the phone on Summers desk started to ring "Detective Summers fourth precinct homicide division, help you?" She listened intently for a long moment and then put her hand over the mouthpiece of the receiver and mouthed the word homicide in Rite's direction. She assured the person on the other end of the phone that they would be on the scene as soon as possible and send them for the information and hung up the phone.

Rite was already in motion, sliding into his jacket and heading for the door. "Where are we headed?" "The Mount Olympus Apartments corner of the Black Pearl on Maple Street. Someone just discovered a DB in one of the units." Well then this could turn out to be a very interesting first day" he shot summer, a sly smile and she asked. "Do you want to drive or shall I?" Rite gave her a curious look. "Unless you have a motorcycle helmet tucked into one of your pockets. I think you had better drive." He said sarcastically. She chuckled to herself. "Isn't it a little too cold to be riding one of those things?" She asked while opening the door to the cruiser. "It's not too bad. Besides, I find a cold wind to the face in the morning to be quite invigorating." He said, ducking into the cruiser and making sure the door was firmly closed and he was buckling his seatbelt as Detective Summer entered into oncoming traffic.

Chapter 3

When they arrived at the scene, which from what Rite could tell was way out of his price range. It was a very high-end apartment complex that could probably only be afforded by doctors and lawyers and high-level business personnel. Rite began taking notice of the environment outside the building and its usual aspects of street-level police work. Setting up the infamous yellow line and controlling the crowd then naturally gathers every time one too many police cars are parked at the same location.

They had not made it very far out of the car when a uniformed police officer came toward them and began explaining the scenario. "It doesn't appear as though it was a robbery as nothing appears to be missing or damaged in any way. And there are no signs of forced entry on the door or any of the Windows. We've already begun to canvass the neighbors to see if there has been any suspicious activity. The victim has been identified as Maggie Simmons. According to her driver's license and a work ID, we found says that she works on a research and development team for White Light pharmaceuticals."

Summer sang to the officer for the information and told him to keep up the good work and to bring any new pertinent information to her straightaway. He assured her that he wanted and then disappeared to continue his work, Summers and Rite walked up two flights of stairs until they arrived at Apartment C. 14. And as they entered, they both noticed that the apartment was in absolutely pristine condition. Almost as if it were a showroom designed to display the virtues of living in this particular apartment building. Rite found this strangely unnerving as it made the scene feel as though it had been staged for their benefit as if it were a training exercise.
The victim lay what appeared to be a very expensive oriental rug "she is certainly well-off judging by the look of this place. Not to mention the rug she's laying on these things aren't cheap." "Research and development scientists are highly prized by pharmaceutical companies as they are the ones responsible for making sure that the drugs do exactly what they're advertised to do. And that they need all the specifications and guidelines set down by the FDA. And since it takes such a long time for a drug to reach the market often 10 to 15 years or more and with millions of dollars at stake pharmaceutical companies don't like to take chances so that development

scientists are very well paid." She said, kneeling down to get a closer look of the body while sliding her left hand into a latex glove.

"You seem to know a lot about the pharmaceutical industry?" Rite said with a semi-raised eyebrow. "I did a year of premed in college before I decided that I would rather study law and criminal justice." Summers said, nonchalantly as if everyone should know exactly what a research and development pharmaceutical scientist does for a living. Rite was kneeling down next to her now putting both his hands into white latex gloves that were stored in a pouch on his belt. "He sniffed the air curiously doesn't this place smell a little too clean to you? Like it has been freshly bleached" Summers nodded. "It reminds me of a hospital, which means one of two things either Ms. Simmons was an exceptionally clean person, or her assailant knew how to cover their tracks. They probably wiped everything in the room down with bleach and ammonia to get rid of any DNA and/or fingerprint evidence. It's probably why she's on the rug as well" Ian thought about it for a moment. "I see what you're getting at; the rug has a lot of deep red colors and being made of natural fibers. Will do an excellent job of absorbing the blood, and then all one would have to do is pour some ammonia and bleach on the rug to destroy any DNA evidence. This individual sure does appear to be smart and motivated and methodical. I hope we don't have a serial killer on our hands." "Me too" Summers said with a sigh.

Just as they begin looking over the numerous knife wounds that were on Mrs. Simmons chest and abdomen. Dr. William Morgan, medical examiner/corner entered the room greeting detective Summers with a subtle. Two finger salute and a smile, rite thought that Dr. Morgan looked like one of those old English country doctors out of a Charles Dickens novel. Or one of those classic Christmas specials, he had a full head of gray hair and a weathered face with deep wrinkles. It looked as though they were the roadmap to a very tough, but interesting life. He had bluish gray eyes that gave the impression that he knew something that no one else did. His classic half frame glasses only intensified this perception.

Dr. Morgan knelt down directly opposite the detectives so he facing them. "A new partner, I see." He said to Summers, using his chin to point in the direction of detective rite as he snapped on his pair of white latex examination gloves. "This is Detective Ian Rite. He came over from the zombie squad, to lend us a hand." She said eyeing Ian with her peripheral vision "well, welcome to homicide detective rite. Hopefully you can keep detective Summers from getting into too much trouble." He said with a half smile. "I will try my best." Ian softly chuckled. "What can you tell us about our victim Doc?" Summers asked almost impatiently. "Judging by the color of the stab wounds, and the pooling of the blood, I would say she has been dead solid five or six hours, but I will know more when I get her back for an autopsy.

And with that Dr. Morgan had a few of the uniformed police officers to lift the body onto a gurney for transport back to the morgue Summers and Rite instructed another uniform to bag and tag the rug as evidence and began to explore the rest of the apartment to find any other clues as to the reason and/or cause of the murder. "Judging by the fact that there was no forced entry and the living room being in pristine condition I'm betting that Simmons knew her attacker. However, it seems strange that other than a few scrapes and cuts on her hands. There was not more defensive wound damage, because no matter how well I know someone if they tried to stab me that many times. You can be damn sure I would put up more of the fight." Rite said, as they ventured down the small hallway toward the bedroom "well, maybe her hands and feet were pinned when the stabbing occurred." "That's a negative ghost rider" -- if that had been the case then it would have been bruising from the rope or duct tape or hands that were incapacitating her." "I see your point, and there was no damage to her head that would indicate that she was knocked unconscious before the stabbing. So what in the hell would make someone so compliant in their own murder?" Summers said, tapping her pen against her notepad repeatedly.

As they entered the bedroom they noticed that it was as neat as the rest of the house and nothing looked out of place. There were a few files scattered on a small desk in the corner next to a laptop. But that did not necessarily indicate that anyone other than Simmons had been there as people often leave folders and forms lying around on their desks next to their laptop for a variety of reasons. However as they glanced at the paperwork they noticed something special about it. It was the side effect report for a drug with the codename (avenging angel). The paperwork detailed the side effects associated with the drug, and it appeared to list the results of a clinical trial of patients on the actual drug, versus those that were on the placebo and as they examined the paperwork closely. They noticed that pages were missing as the first few pages were labeled one through three and then jump down to nine and 10 "there is a discrepancy in the files on the desk. I think maybe somehow, the information that was in this report is linked to the murder of Ms. Simmons" "maybe it has something to do with the results of the clinical trials with the results of the clinical trials, if the drug wasn't holding up to its expectations. There would be plenty of reason, to falsify a report and motivated murder as white star pharmaceuticals could potentially lose hundreds of millions of dollars in sales and research if it was shown that there was something wrong with the drug I also think we should have our tech guys take a look at the laptop. Maybe they can find some information that will lead us to the exact motive and/or killer" Summers said.

We should see if we can find her cell phone as well the call log will have the last people she called. Maybe one of them can supply us with some pertinent information." "Or maybe one of them is the killer" Summers said with a sarcastic chuckle. (If only it were that easy Rite thought, but then my job would be boring as it would be really easy to catch the bad guys).

Chapter 4

As they rode back to the station the detectives exchange theories about just who would stand directly to gain if a pharmaceutical researcher like maybe Simmons was killed. They talked all sorts of theories back and forth like someone was blackmailing Simmons into falsifying records for financial gain, or someone at the drug company felt as though the job might be lost if the drug failed. But none of their theories seem to make any sense. As far as maybe Simmons was concerned. She didn't have any real authority and couldn't stop the drug from being manufactured on her own. And she was not responsible for the drug trials themselves. The only thing that even remotely made any sense was someone wanting the information about the trials and was willing to kill to hide it from the world.

When they got into the office Rite called the phone company to see how soon they could send over a copy of Maggie's phone records so that he and Simmons could run down some leads on the case. They said they would have been sent over ASAP. Right was surprised that all he had to do was ask. He didn't have to threaten anyone, or twist the arm. All he had to do was say he was a police officer and verify his badge number with the phone company. He smiled to himself (this is definitely going to be different than the zombie squad). Shortly after he hung up the phone, a young kid who looked like he would be more at home playing Dungeons & Dragons. He placed Maggie's laptop on the desk directly in between Rite and Summers. "I got into the laptop and checked her e-mail accounts. There was nothing suspicious in the e-mails, no threats or anything of that nature. However, a recent correspondence indicated that she had been talking to Mark Callahan on a Semi-regular basis. I couldn't tell you, what about as the messages themselves have been deleted. But either Ms. Simmons or someone else forgot to delete the e-mail registry "why does that name sound so familiar?" Rite asked Summers. "Because he's a reporter for the Seattle Sun he does all sorts of exposés on political and corporate corruption, and anything else he feels that he can use to get a reaction from the public." The tech kid cleared his throat. "You should also know that there have been a significant number of files that have been deleted from this computer. I can't tell you, if it was done by Ms. Simmons herself or if someone else did it for her, but I can tell you that they were fairly large files, and then they must have been important, because they were at one point, protected by a separate password" rite and

Summers thanked the kid for the information. He told them they were welcome, and that he would turn the computer into the evidence locker. Once more now that he was finished with it.

We should definitely see what this Mark Callahan has to say about what Maggie was up to: a few hours later. They manage to get a hold of Mark Callahan left are being told of Maggie's murder, assured the police detectives that he would help in whatever way he possibly could, he informed the detectives that he would drop by the station tomorrow afternoon and answer whatever questions they wanted. He would have done it right away, except he was on assignment, and by the time. He was finished, it would be too late to do anything productive, and as he sounded genuinely and disturbed to hear about the murder. Right was pretty sure that he would report to the station as promised. Tomorrow afternoon, and if he didn't it would not be that hard to find them again. Besides which he also mentioned he had received a message from Maggie in which she sounded like she had something important to tell them about her research or something to do with a pharmaceutical company. He told the detective that they were supposed to meet at their favorite coffee shop. The next morning at 10:00 AM, and now he waited for an hour and she had never shown up. And Rite figured if he had committed the murder. He would not be telling him that he had recently received a message from the victim in which she sounded distressed.

Rite, and Summers spent the rest of the day going over Maggie's phone records and the only other number that stuck out to the detectives was the number for a Mr. Brian Fillmore, who was apparently Maggie's supervisor in the research and development lab at White Light. She had made several calls, the longest one lasting 35 minutes. Two days before she had left an interesting message for Mark Callahan. The detectives contacted Brian Fillmore and he too agreed to be as helpful as he could with the investigation. He sounds just as surprised and shocked as Mr. Callahan when he was told that Maggie had been murdered.

It was late, so Summers and Rite decided to knock off for the evening and hopefully achieve a fresh perspective on the case in the morning as Rite knew from experience that things tended to look a lot clearer after a good night's rest and a strong cup of coffee. And as he was zipping up his motorcycle jacket and heading for the front door of the station Summers in tow. She said "I still can't get over this case. I understand the drug being worth enough to kill over what I don't understand how someone can just lay still, while being stabbed 14 times. It makes absolutely no sense." "I know, but there has to be a reason for it medical or otherwise. Maybe Dr. Morgan will be able to shed some light on it for us in the morning." He said as he held the station door open for Summers, she gave him a wink as she passed through it "I guess chivalry is not dead." "Nope, it's just semi-retired." They both laughed.

Rite began to slide his hands into his old black leather riding gloves as they got closer to his mechanical steed he had his helmet perched precariously on the back of his head. To accomplish this task he had ironically parked only two stalls away from Summers own car. She was standing beside him, directly in front of his machine, which was a triumph that had been modified to resemble the café racers of the 1940s and 50s that were made popular in Great Britain. It was designed for speed similar to modern sport bikes with a more classic design element. "I can't believe you ride this thing. I always thought they were dangerous" she said with a curious look and a slightly concerned tone in her voice. Rite smiled. "After working for zombie squad, riding this thing is like getting a hug from a giant friendly teddy bear, besides. Scientists have said that when you are riding a motorcycle. Your brain thinks you are flying like Superman. So I guess you could say for 45 minutes twice a day. I am Superman" this made her smile. "Just be careful on that thing. I don't want to have to break in a new partner anytime soon." She said, heading towards their own car rite assured her that he would be fine, swung his leg over the machine pulled his helmet down tight closed the visor turned the key and the machine roared to life as the light had woken at Dragon from his slumber. He cracked up to throttle a few times to check the response and bring up the RPMs gave Summers. A two fingered salute, which she returned in the rearview mirror, and then he was off into the darkness.

Chapter 5

Ian truly did feel as though he was flying like Superman. When he was on his machine, particularly at night when the roads were quiet and clear of traffic, and there was no sound other than that of his trusty steed in its British racing green paint scheme with its chrome fenders and 900 CC engine with its deep, low growl that was reminiscent Rite always thought of a tiger preparing to pounce, although it was definitely a dragon when it first woke up he thought with a satisfactory smile. Underneath his helmet this machine often helped him to put his life into perspective. It allowed him some personal time, where no part of the real world could intrude. It seemed to make all the stress of the day melt away into nothingness almost as though his stress could not keep up with the speed of the machine.

He also did his best thinking on his machine he often thought about Jenni and what she was doing in New York writing copy for that big high-level ad agency she worked for, he wondered how many advertisements he had seen lately that she had done the design and slogan for this thought made Rite smile as he felt he got to see a little piece of her all over the city every day.

They had really tried to make it work and for a few magical months it had, she even moved to Seattle to be with him. But as he had predicted a genetic experience is not a good basis for two people to engage in a romantic relationship. Especially when that individual is a deep undercover police officer, who can be away for weeks or even months at a time may be even years. So after about six months they both decided that maybe what they needed was space and she'd gone back to New York to resume her career in advertisement and he had asked for a transfer to homicide. It was not as though they had officially ended their relationship. It was more like a trial separation, applying the philosophy that if something is truly yours and the universe will make sure it comes back to you. He still secretly hoped one day this philosophy would prove to be true, because he had never felt about anyone who we felt about Jenni it was as if she even made breathing easier. He still talked to her on a semi-regular basis as she was easy to talk to, and he felt like she truly understood him on a deep level and adjust the sound of her voice was therapeutic. Almost as good if not better than riding on his machine.

He leaned into the final corner that would lead him up the street to his apartment. And as he neared his driveway he pressed a button on his keychain to open his garage door. He let off the gas so he could coast into the garage without disturbing his neighbors anymore than necessary. Once he was securely in the garage he pushed the button on the keychain once more, and closed the garage door and turned the key in the ignition off and put the Dragon and Tiger to sleep once more. Flipping out the kickstand and gently leaning to one side the kickstand made a satisfactory (thump) on the concrete floor of the garage, signifying that the day's work was truly done. He sat there for a moment still straddling the machine without removing his helmet or gloves and let out a deep breath and shook his head gently from side to side and rolled his shoulders as if trying to make sure that none of the negative aspects of his police work were going to follow him into his house. He knew this was impossible, but it was worth a shot.

Satisfied that he was relaxed enough to enter his home. He removed his gloves, and then his helmet and removed the keys from the ignition and went through an inside garage door that led into the living room. He stopped at a small wooden liquor cabinet, which his father had built many years ago, and laid his go bag that contained all of his necessary extra detective equipment like notepads, extra crime scene gloves, police baton, a few extra magazines of ammunition, CS spray, and even a spare shirt because he never knew when these little extras might come in handy. He placed his gloves and helmet on top of the cabinet next to his bag and then opened a drawer that contained a specialized rubber pad on which his pistol would rest, he removed the pistol from its holster, worked at the action removing a round from the chamber and removed the magazine put the bullet back in the magazine and placed the magazine and weapon next to each other on the rubber pad and closed the drawer. He hung his leather jacket and shoulder holster in a closet right next to the liquor cabinet he untucked his shirt from his jeans opened up the main doors on the liquor cabinet and removed a bottle of Jamison's 18-year-old single malt, as well as a highball glass into which he poured about three fingers of whiskey placing the cork back in the bottle and put the bottle back into the cabinet and casually walked into the kitchen and over to the automatic water dispenser contained within the refrigerator door as he had learned years ago from his father that just a little bit of water in the whiskey would help to unlock all of its flavor. With this accomplished, he turned his attention to his personal phone lying on the kitchen counter, he never carried his personal phone on duty because he was not willing to risk anyone else gaining access to it.

He checked the voicemail box. He was surprisingly happy that there was a message from Jenni. He took the phone and his whiskey over to his favorite easy chair so that he could fully enjoy the relaxing experience of playing her message and hearing her voice. Once he was sure he was as comfortable as he was going to get a hit the play button on the message and put the phone on speaker and leaned back and closed his eyes.

"Hello, my handsome Marine (Rite still could not get over the sound of her voice. It made him feel as though you were the only person other than her in the entire world). I hope you are having fun, arresting bad guys and you are keeping out of trouble as much as possible, at least that you are not getting shot at on a regular basis. Hopefully you are adjusting well to being a regular detective. I'm sure you are, as there is nothing you can't do when you put your mind to it. As far as me goes, I am doing all right. We picked up a very large and lucrative ad campaign today and I got to be the lead designer. So go me. And if this project goes well, I am hoping they will make me lead on a few others which may eventually lead to a promotion. Anyway, as I say, I hope you are well and that your universes balance. I miss your face and will talk to you soon. I love you" and with that the message ended Rite disconnected the call pulled the lever to recline the easy chair finished the last of the whiskey in the class, placing it on the end table beside the chair, closed his eyes and imagined Jenni laying next to him, wrapped in each other's arms, submerged in an ocean of love. This was his last thought before he fell asleep.

Chapter 6

Rite awoke at 4 AM the next morning to the realization that he had fallen asleep in his chair when he only intended to rest his eyes for a moment and realized that he would be unable to return to sleep, because once he was awake that was the end of it. It was a habit he had developed as a Marine, because no matter what time a Marine wakes up. They have to be ready for anything. He also had a very good internal clock, and if he taught himself to wake up at five in the morning. Then he was going to wake up at five in the morning.

Although he had not intended to wake up this early he figured he might as well get an early start on the day as they were going to be interviewing Mark Callahan about the phone call that Maggie Simmons had made to him right before she had died. And Ian figured that it never hurt to get a little extra jump on his police work. So he went through his morning routine, and he and his machine were in the parking lot of the station house at a quarter after six in the morning.

He was pouring himself another cup of coffee at 8 AM, according to the clock on the wall, when Summers walked into the squad room. "You're here kind of early this morning a little gung ho about your police work eh?" She said with a smile. "Sure thing I have been on the premises since 6:15 AM" "Jesus. I mean, I like being a cop as much as the next girl but I'm not getting up at 5 AM, unless it's a diehard emergency. What's the matter couldn't sleep or just really excited about your secondary as a homicide detective?" She said with a smirk. "Actually, a friend woke me up at around 4 AM this morning and after that. I just couldn't get back to sleep." "That must be some friend; I wish I had a friend that would wake me up at four in the morning." She said with an inquisitive look that only a curious woman can pull off. Rite smiled sarcastically. "If it was that sort of situation I would not have been here so early, as I would not have any extra energy left over that would need to be burnt off." His smile grew a little wider, Summers gave him a playful shove in the shoulder and he rocked to one side making a big show of how she had interrupted him in the middle of fixing his coffee.

"Well I hope next time your friend wakes you up at four in the morning she can help you burn off some of that excess energy." She said as she stirred some brown sugar into her coffee. "Me too" Rite said thoughtfully. "We ought to go be detectives now. Dr. Morgan should be in and maybe he will have some insight as to why someone would remain still in active in their own stabbing." She said as she took us a coffee Rite agreed that may be true to autopsy was just what he needed to get his detectives juices flowing they took the elevator down to the basement level, where the autopsy examination room is located and they entered the room to find Dr. Morgan intently fixated on a microscope Detective Summers cleared her throat to gain his attention. He looked up semi-startled with these glasses resting on the tip of his nose pushed them back up into their proper place, with his index finger so that he could get a proper visual on who was standing in his autopsy suite. Once his vision was made clear again with a sly smile he said "good morning detectives, to what do I owe the pleasure of this early morning visit? For some new and exciting information about our murder victim Maggie Simmons, is that the correct assumption?" "Indeed it is Dr." Simmons said returning the doctors warm greeting in the form of a smile. "As a matter of fact, I did manage to find something interesting for you and your partner." He said pointing with his chin in Rite's direction. "At this acknowledgment Rite gave a two fingered salute from above the left eyebrow "the stab wounds on our victim appeared to be window dressing. Most of them are superficial, at best, and the ones that might have done some damage appeared to be post-mortem." Rite and Summers stared at each other as if they did not quite understand exactly what they were being told "what do you mean they were superficial", Summers asked in a very curious, almost weary voice. "Exactly that most of these wounds are superficial, meaning nonlethal, particularly the ones on the chest and stomach, as are most of the ones close to the neck and collarbone. That is, all except for these two. (He drew a gloved finger across to the carotid artery in the throat). But as I say, this was done postmortem. Almost as if it were an afterthought, which is what I believe all the stab wounds to be merely camouflage." "Camouflage?" both the detective said in unison with the same amount of surprise in her voice. Dr. Morgan took a breath and said "yes, I believe the stabbing was designed to camouflage the real cause of death (and before the detectives could ask what that was). Dr. Morgan pointed to a very small, perfectly round wound that looked like it could have been made by a bee sting). "This is the mark left behind by any kind of intravenous injection needle." He said pointing to the spot on the lower part of Maggie's right collarbone. "I almost missed it myself. And if I had not decided to examine the body one more time to be extra sure that I had accounted for every mark. I probably would have." "What do you think she was injected with Dr.?"

Rite asked in a surprisingly casual tone. "I don't think she was injected detective. I know she was. She was injected with adrenaline a common practice during cardiac arrest procedures in hospitals to prevent the heart from stopping altogether. But if too much is used, it will have the opposite effect and will cause the heart to work overtime and eventually burn itself out,"

"So you're saying she was deliberately injected with an overdose of adrenaline to make it look like a heart attack or some other heart related medical problem" that is correct Detective. Dr. Morgan said, with no great emphasis. "And how do you know, it was adrenaline. Specifically, that was used?" "Because detective it takes time for adrenaline to metabolize in the body and Ms. Simmons died before this could be completed."

"But who would have access to pure adrenaline in enough quantity to inject some and stop her heart?" Summer said to no one in particular, and Rite looked at Summers, knowingly and said "someone that works at a pharmaceutical company." Summers gave him a sheepish look as if to say (I can't believe I didn't get that). Summer said. "I see your obvious point, but don't they place tracking numbers and barcodes on substances used by pharmaceuticals and hospitals? So wouldn't someone notice a missing vial of adrenaline missing?" Rite said. "Not necessarily. I mean, pharmaceutical companies have thousands of vials of all sorts of stuff going in and out of their labs on a daily basis. It would be easy enough for something to get lost, or even to doctor a report about the amount of a particular shipment." Dr. Morgan cleared his throat once again and said "detectives. While I do enjoy a good theory and that is a sound theory of investigation by the way. It is not have to be as complicated as that, as there is enough adrenaline in Epinephrine pen. To achieve the desired result, they are available at most local pharmacies and are available with a prescription or in certain cases. Simply proof of a medical diagnosis for severe allergies which would be far less complicated than doctoring a shipping report and far less inconspicuous and even far easier to use. As these devices are designed to be used by anyone even the patient during an emergency it doesn't even take that much force to apply the injection merely a few pounds of pressure."

"That's very interesting information Doctor, it could be that someone wanted to give Ms. Simmons, what they thought would be untraceable death. Or maybe even a painless and quick death, and then realized it would appear very strange. If someone so young and healthy, died of a heart attack, although it does happen occasionally without prior health issues, it would be very strange indeed. So the subject had the brilliant idea of stabbing Ms. Simmons in hopes of distracting us from the real cause of death. By not only covering up the injection site with the wounds but also because they figured with such an obvious COD may be the medical examiner would not look too close during the autopsy." "My thoughts exactly detective" Dr. Morgan said with a slight congratulatory tone in his voice as if to say. Good job on your first case).

"Lucky for us that Dr. Morgan is so thorough." Summers gave him a wink and which he tipped an invisible hat and returned the wink. "I just couldn't get over how clean the majority of the apartment was ordinarily was, ordinarily, when someone is stabbed at many times is usually a crime of passion, and/or robbery, but there is always a significant struggle and the fact that this crime scene didn't have any of those features kept eating at me. So I took a second look with a fine tooth comb, and viola, here you are." "It seems that our murderer was so concerned about not leaving any of their DNA or other evidence behind that they were too careful. Almost to the point of paranoia, and therefore may have given us the very clue we need to solve the case" Rite said with a tone of satisfaction. That summer seemed to return with a nod. "Well thank you very much for your insights. Dr. Morgan. We appreciate them a great deal." Summers said. "Anytime Detective, more than happy to help and after saying their goodbyes, and thanks once more, the detectives boarded the elevator and returned to the squad room.

It had been roughly 8:15 AM, when they had entered into their diatribe with Dr. Morgan and learned to be very interesting information. It was almost 9 AM, and they knew in an hour or so, they would be able to reach Mr. Mark Callahan and bring him into answer a few questions about just what he and Mrs. Simmons were discussing over the course of many phone calls.

Detective Rite managed to get a hold of Mr. Callahan, who agreed to arrive at the station promptly at 10:30 AM to answer whatever questions were put to him so that they could solve the murder of Maggie Simmons. And a 10:30 AM on the nose he was in the station inquiring with the desk sergeant about where Detective Simmons and right might be, as he had an appointment the desk sergeant had one of his civilian aides escort Mr. Callahan into the squad room and present him to Detectives Rite and Simmons.

Mark Callahan cordially introduced himself and shook hands with each of the detectives in turn. Each time reiterating that he was willing to do whatever was necessary to help them solve the murder of Maggie Simmons. The detectives escorted him into a conference room area, rather than an interrogation room, because at this point he was voluntarily presenting himself, and there was not any serious indication that he might be a suspect. However, if the course of the conversation changed detective Rite would not hesitate, to place Mr. Calhoun in handcuffs and shipped from the venue of the conversation from the relatively pleasant surroundings of the conference room to that of the stark surroundings of an interrogation room.

Detective Simmons offered Mark Callahan a choice of beverages, of which he declined. So she took out her notebook and pen and place them on the table in front of her and then informed Mark that he was not under arrest or an oath of any kind, and he was voluntarily cooperating in an ongoing police investigation. She also informed him that this conversation would be recorded in case there was some information that might later prove to be valuable, he confirmed that he understood that he was not in any way obligated to be conducting this meeting with the detectives, as well as gave his consent for the recording of the conversation.

Simmons started things off. "Did you know Simmons on a personal level as well as professional or just a professional level?" Mark replied "it was more personal than professional. By that I mean we've known each other since college we used to be roommates. We've been dating for a few years, but we've been good friends ever since. She typically doesn't help me with my stories as I focused mostly on political corruption and the like. But recently, she had been sending me messages about the possibility that some of the test results for the drug that was going to severely repress if not cure the symptoms of MS. We exchanged some e-mails discussing the possibility of taking this information public and the writing an exposé in the event that she found out that someone was deliberately tampering with the information being generated by the research study.

I didn't think much it at first, but she started calling me more and more frequently, telling me that something just wasn't right. As a matter of fact, the morning she was found in her apartment. She had insisted that we meet for coffee at our favorite shop. She said she had something seemingly important to show me that would prove it. Someone had been tampering with the data being generated by the study, and that the drug had some major side effects and was not ready for public consumption by any means at the time. I just thought maybe she had calmed down and realized it wasn't as serious as she had initially thought. Or maybe she was distracted by further investigations and had forgotten about our appointment. So I didn't think anything of being stood up at the time however now I am absolutely sure that whatever she sounded during her research had something to do with her death."

Detective Rite asked Calhoun, "Did Maggie ever mention anyone in particular that could possibly be the culprit behind the tampering with the results of this study. Or anyone who might have motivation for doing so?" "No, she never mentioned anyone in particular that she thought might have been behind the tampering. Just that she was fairly certain that it happened. I guess she figured if I ran exposé in an investigation was sure to follow. And then the person would be found out and brought to justice, but I guess there won't be any exposé. As I never got to see the information that Maggie had dug up." He sounded as if he were going to tear up at any moment "I can't imagine anyone wanting to hurt Maggie. She would never hurt a fly. When we were in college, she volunteered to go to Africa for a year to help with disease prevention and education programs. She went into medicine, with the intention of helping people. It was this passion to help others. That led her into the research and development side of medicine, because she figured rather than treating one patient at a time. Being a doctor or a surgeon, developing medications would allow her to help millions of people all over the world simultaneously. She was one of the best people I have ever had the pleasure of knowing." He said with tears trickling down his cheeks.

Simmons handed him some tissues, and he thanked her and apologized for the tears. "You never realize how much you love someone or how big of an impact they have on your life until they're gone. I really loved her. She was the one that secretly inspired me to take on this type of journalism. She was my way of helping the world to better itself but rather than using medicine I guess I used words), he said somberly. "Are you absolute sure that she did not mention anyone specifically, that could possibly have a grudge against White Light pharmaceuticals or that would benefit from Maggie's murder and the data being repressed?" Summers asked in an encouraging yet motherly tone. "No, there is no one specific that you mentioned even in passing, but anyone in the research and development division, or anyone in the company for that matter, could have reason to want to see the drug push through as it would result in a serious financial loss for the company as drugs takes such a long time to develop. So anyone of interested in seeing the drug on the market from pharmaceutical distributors to doctors, could have orchestrated the blackmail and/or repression of the studies to ensure their financial gain or whatever end goal they had came to fruition."

"All I know for certain is that Maggie was not only worried about the data being tampered with. But that there were extreme side effects to this particular drug that could result in the premature death of anyone who took the drug of that I'm certain."

Detective Simmons asked "do you know what any of these side effects might be?" Mark thought for a moment and then said. "She did mention a few of the e-mails that she had noticed a decrease in the white blood cell count of certain patients, as well as problems with the kidneys when it came to filtering the leftover remnants of the drug out of the body system, but at the time she made it sound as though it wasn't a serious problem and could be remedied before the drug went online. But if you have questions about the drug itself and deal might be susceptible to blackmail, you should talk to Brian Fillmore. He was her supervisor in the lab, and they were all so very close friends as a matter of fact. He was a professor when Maggie and I were at university. He taught most of her premed classes he is also the reason many ended up working at white star pharmaceuticals. He began working for them are senior year after retiring from teaching, and when we graduated. He wrote, Maggie, a glowing recommendation that got her hired right out of school."

Simmons scribbled some notes in her note pad and asked Mark. "Is there anyone else that you can think of anyone that might know Maggie and Brian Fillmore?" Mark couldn't think of anyone like that. And after a few more basic questions, the detectives thanked him for his time. And Summers gave him a business card and said "if you happen to think of anything else that you feel might be important for you to not hesitate to call." He took the card and assured them that if he thought of anything else that might be of value he would not hesitate to call both the detectives.

Although Rite just couldn't help but feel that they were missing something the crime scene was too clean. Everyone makes at least one mistake, whether it's a shoe print. A dropped receipt doesn't matter, but they always make one somewhere, somehow, someway and he was pretty sure that the perpetrator of this latest case had as well as of yet. However, Rite was unsure exactly what, was this perpetrator was very good indeed, whoever they were they even cleaned in Maggie's fingernails. To make sure that there was no DNA or other microfiber evidence in point of fact. The only major was the blood stains on the rug and those only help determine how long she had been dead from the size of the blood pool and the spread patterns. It was as if the perpetrator was drawing deliberate attention to the blood stains, as well as the stab wounds. Just like Doc Morgan said, to distract the detectives, detention. Keep them focused on the body and not much else, because Rite was pretty sure that if the real focus of the murder was Maggie Simmons and make killer as clean as they were would have definitely cleaned up all the blood evidence as well.

Sitting at his desk Rite suddenly had a very sickening thought they'd made him feel as though there was a cold steel bowling ball in the pit of this gut (son of a Bitch!), He said under his breath, just loud enough for Summers ears to perk up (what if the perpetrator is a cop?!), He said low. Under his breath almost as if you were uttering a curse, Summers leaned forward in her chair so that you are almost lying across her desk. And then noses were almost touching she looked him deep in the eyes and growled. "Did you just say, what I think you just said?" In a tone so low only a dog could hear "that is dangerous territory. You are treading in partner that is a whole other can of worms, which involves a whole other type of investigation. On top of the one we are to have." Rite did not break her gaze for a second. He just brought his voice even lower than it already was and said "I am completely aware of what kind of territory I am treading in. I spent a long time operating in very dangerous territory, and I don't want to be here anymore than you do, but we have to look at all possible options. And this would explain a lot, if they were caught they would know our procedures, and exactly how we collect evidence and how to get rid of it. I'm not saying they're a cop now, but maybe they were, hell they don't even have to be a cop they could be a former forensic scientist that now works in the private sector for a pharmaceutical company or distribution organization. These are possibilities, I really think we should explore" Summers gave a sigh of defeat, because she knew she could not get him off this train of thought and then reluctantly said. "All right, but if we are going to pursue this line of questioning then let's keep it on the down low until we have some concrete and steel evidence accusing a cop and/or forensic scientist is not something any department is going to take lightly even if they are a former investigator." Rite wholeheartedly agreed that that would be the best plan of action for now at least until as she put it; they had some concrete and steel evidence to back up their theory.

Rite decided that until they had the evidence they required. He would keep their digging into this particular subject strictly to an after-hours endeavor. He didn't think anyone would pay much attention to a cop spending is evening hours digging through old records and case files. As many cops had a pet cold case. They worked on during their off-duty hours. It was usually a case they couldn't solve or at least not to their satisfaction, and it nagged at them and became the thing they did when they couldn't sleep. Like smoking a cigarette or drinking a warm glass of milk every cop had one. Whether they admit it or not.

Chapter 7

The next day at around 2:30 in the afternoon Brian Fillmore and his wife Maxine (Max for short) presented themselves to Detective Rite and Summers to answer whatever questions the detectives wish them too so that they might help the progress of the investigation into Maggie Simmons murder. Brian Fillmore and his wife Maxine entered the conference room with Brian Fillmore, looking as one would expect a research scientist to look and long thin features and Rite could tell from his pale complexion that he was more at home in the lab than anywhere else. He was a new breed of scientist and/or technology developer. That Rite likes to think of as (geek chic). This was the age of humanity. When the power of a man's brains were worth more than the power of his muscles and Rite could tell Brian Fillmore was taking full advantage of his newfound affluence, because although Rite was still very sure that Mr. Fillmore was holding on very tightly to his hard-core geek status. He was a hard-core geek, in an expensive suit.

And as Rite were shaking hands with Mr. Fillmore and thanking him for coming and for his willingness to cooperate and/or assist the investigation. He couldn't help but notice that Maxine Fillmore look like the ultimate high powered geek status symbol of the trophy wife. She looked to be about 5'8" tall (without the high heels). She was a brunette with hazel eyes and a physique that might have come from a former Olympic swimmer or Swedish Bikini team, Rite could not decide which end he suspected that she was far smarter and aware of things than she was letting on, right thought she was trying to play the role of a trophy wife but carried herself with an air of confidence. It was difficult to fake and keep hidden, although she tried, but Rite just couldn't see why. He knew that she was part of the drug company that her husband worked for and was far more than a secretary. He assumed she was just trying to play the part that society expected her to play, because it was easier to work with the system and against it. These suspicions were confirmed as Rite said. "If you don't mind we are going to record this conversation, just in case we need to refer anything later in the investigation. You are in no way under any obligation to participate in this meeting. You're not being charged with a crime, and you are here of your own free will. Is that correct?" (Please state yes or no for the record). They both answered "yes" almost in unison and then Maxine Fillmore added. "I have already informed my husband of the standard procedures such as these that take place during a murder investigation. And I can assure you, we will not impede your investigation in any way." At this revelation, Summers and Rite shot each other sideways glance with slightly raised eyebrows.

"I used to be a lawyer in case you're wondering how I know so much about the standard operating procedures of a murder investigation, although I am no longer practicing as a member of a firm. I do occasionally help my husband's company with their legal matters. As a privately contracted attorney, so feel free to be as frank as possible detectives. I'm not shy, and neither is my husband."

Detective Summers began the conversation by asking "did you or your husband know Ms. Simmons outside of a working environment?" Of course we did Detective. We've made no secret about that. It's common knowledge that my husband taught most of Maggie's premed courses. When she was at the university as a matter of fact, she was my husband's teaching assistant for several years. That is until he retired from teaching to go into medical research as he felt he could do more good developing a medication directly rather than teaching a bunch of students. That would not be ready to contribute to the medical field for a number of years (the whole time. Brian Fillmore was nodding in agreement). Over the years Maggie became like the daughter we never had as she spent so much time in Brian's classes as a student. And then assisting him with others she had dinner with us on a regular basis. She would on occasion when working late nights with Brian use the spare bedroom." So just to clarify, Summers said. "You would consider Maggie then, to be part of the family?" "That is absolutely correct detective as I have previously stated she would like the daughter we never had." She said in a very lawyers' tone (Brian Fillmore nodded once more in agreement).

Maxine Fillmore continued. "That's why when Maggie finished her education. Brian helped her to get a foothold with the company by hiring her as his data verification technician (fact checker) for his team and within a few years she had worked your way up to the position she currently holds (excuse me) held, which is/was assistant project manager. Basically second-in-command after Brian (Brian Fillmore nodded once more in agreement) and their team was on the verge of making some real breakthroughs before Maggie's unfortunate accident (at this statement Brian Fillmore began to fidget with his ring as though he were trying to hold back tears and Maxine reached over and put her arm around his shoulders and squeezed gently) we just can't believe that something like this would happen to Maggie. I mean, she was the sweetest, most compassionate person I ever met. She was always willing to go the extra mile to help someone in need. The kind of person that doesn't even realize they're doing a good deed. When they do it if you know what I mean." Rite directed his questions at Brian Fillmore. "We know from your phone records. Mr. Fillmore that Maggie called you a considerable number of times in the days leading up to her unfortunate accident would you mind telling me what those phone calls were about?"

Brian Fillmore hesitated for a second as if collecting his thoughts looked at his wife as if seeking reassurance (she gently squeezed his shoulders once more). He took a deep breath and said "she had been calling me and insisting that something was wrong with the data being generated by the control study for the drug. And then it had been tampered with, and the drug had considerable more side effects than initially thought. And I tried to reassure her that no one in or outside the company had tampered with the data from this study and that the drug was progressing on schedule, and any minor complications that remained would be worked out before the drug went to market. But she was absolutely insistent that something was wrong with the drug, and this study needed to be re-examined at a base level (starting from scratch), which would mean delaying the release of the drug by several months. Maybe even years, I assured her that this was unnecessary as our company always maintains the highest quality standards but I did agree to take a look at the data for my base level one more time. She said that she'd found some discrepancies in a file, and one of them resolved before we went any further. Unfortunately she died before she could show me the suspicious files with the discrepancy. And when I checked, the information contained in the case study I could not find any such discrepancies, and I thoroughly check, detectives believe you me, allegations such as these are no laughing matter."

Summers scribbled in her notebook, and then asked no one in particular. "Can you think of anyone in particular, that may receive a direct benefit from the information Maggie had not seeing the light of day?" Brian Fillmore responded "no detective. I cannot everyone on my team was dedicated as myself and Maggie to developing not a cure directly in at least a medication that would severely lessen the symptoms of MS and allow patients to live a better quality of life longer than ever before." Summers scribbled more in her notebook took a sip from the bottle of water. She had on the table, and then said. "Isn't it true that if the data you had on the drug I believe you referred to it as avenging angel was proven to be incorrect that your company would stand to lose millions, possibly billions in revenue, while the drug is being revamped?"

"Yes that is true the company would lose a significant sum of money. If the drug had to be reengineered but that would be a drop in the bucket compared to the financial losses, we would suffer from the lawsuits we would incur from patients. If the drug was put on the market and was potentially lethal, so detectives it is far better to be safe than sorry and especially when the company has a reputation of such high-quality as White Light pharmaceuticals does. We are one of the most trusted names in medicine, worldwide. And risking the company's 75 year global reputation for quality is simply not worth the inconveniences caused by reengineering one drug, particularly one that may only act as a suppressant and not a cure." (At this Max squirmed in her chair as if she were physically demonstrating her disagreement).

Detective Rite said "the fact that you your self have no moral qualms about reengineering the drug and pushing its development back months or even years in order to assure the safety of the American public and avoid tarnishing your companies stellar reputation is very admirable. Mr. Fillmore, but that doesn't mean that there is not someone willing to do whatever is necessary to make sure the drug passes the FDA inspection so that it can start being consumed by the public.

Fillmore adjusted his tie, cleared his throat and said "I have no doubt that other companies have such unscrupulous people working for them detective. But I can assure you that no one on my team would be willing to commit murder just to make sure that avenging angel is approved for public use and further development."

Brian Fillmore was extremely adamant on that point to the point his face began to turn slightly red. As if he was trying very hard to suppress his anger. The detectives asked him and Mrs. Fillmore a few more cursory questions and then shook hands once more and thank them for their time Rite gave Fillmore one of his business cards and told him that, should he think of anything else, however small that might be relevant to the investigation he should not hesitate to call, he also told Brian Fillmore that he might be needed to report back to the station in necessary during the course of the investigation. He reassured the Detective that he would be happy to report whenever necessary. And then he and Mrs. Fillmore headed for the exit and the rest of their day.

Rite glanced at Summers "Did you see how Maxine Fillmore was squirming in her chair, when her husband mentioned that no single drug was worth risking his company's reputation and profits for. I got the feeling she was having a hard time swallowing that statement" Summers returned the knowing glance and said "I noticed that as well. She was definitely thinking about something and it was not the outstanding reputation of her husband's company, I also got the feeling and I can't really explain why that she knew a little bit more about the medical profession, and she was letting on, her husband used to be a professor after all. Maybe she knows a little bit more about this avenging angel, than we think."

Rite said, I think we should look into Mrs. Fillmore's background. Just a little bit more and find out exactly what she omitted from the conversation. Of course I'll do it as discreetly as possible so as not to arouse any unwanted attention to ourselves."

Rite and Summers spent the rest of the day checking into Brian Fillmore's research and development teams at White Light pharmaceuticals all the team members had clean records and that was no evidence to suggest that any of them were being blackmailed or financially compensated for altering the research data of the drug. They conducted their background research on the team late into the evening, until finally there was no amount of caffeine that would keep Summer's eyelids from drooping, and she suggested to Rite that they call it a night and start fresh in the morning, he told her to have a good night. But that he was going to stay and do a little research as there was something about Mrs. Fillmore that was not sitting right with him and he would have to scratch this itch before he could possibly get any sleep. She looked at him and said "you're like a dog with a bone. Once you get your teeth into something you just don't like go." He just smiled and said "that's why they pay me the big bucks."

Summers grabbed her coat and a few folders from her desk and with a yawn that would make Rip van Winkle proud said. "Don't stare at those pages too long, otherwise you'll go blind. And if you do decide to go home on that man machine of yours, ride safe and keep the rubber side on the road as I really don't want to go shopping for a new partner." Rite gave her a wink and a smile and said that he promised not to go blind. And not to become an organ donor, and with that Summers disappeared for the night.

Chapter 8

The squad room was virtually a ghost town with only the dust bunnies and one lone janitor for company, and Rite was still hunched over his desk with a stack of records having to do with Maxine and Brian Fillmore. He was looking for anything that was even remotely relevant to the case. And he was about ready to surrender for the night when he suddenly noticed two very unusual things. One happened to be Maxine Fillmore's college records which stated that she had been pre-med. But after graduation, rather than doing her residency and furthering her medical career like most students in her major, she had decided to switch gears entirely, and pursue a career in law and in the other strange thing he saw in her transcripts that her maiden name was Murphy and her father was listed as Daniel Murphy and on a gut feeling he cross-referenced, Daniel Murphy, with old police roll call records. Not expecting to find anything in particular, he just had a hunch that he had heard that name before, but could not remember where and to his astonishment there was a Daniel Murphy, in the records; he had been part of the crime scene investigations unit all the way from the 70s to the early 90s before retiring, and taking his pension and moving to Florida. Like so many other retired cops before him.

This revelation in information of course in no way directly indicated that Mrs. Fillmore had any direct involvement in the murder of Maggie Simmons but Ian was not the type of Detective to believe in coincidences, the universe was just entirely too small. In his opinion anyway, he decided that since it was getting close to 3:30 AM he should probably go home and get at least a few hours of solid rack time. He gathered up all his necessary essentials and the folders on Brian and Maxine Fillmore, as well as her father's service record. He thought they might make for some interesting bedtime reading. He tucked them into his rucksack, slid into his riding leathers and checked the chamber of his weapon to make sure he did not contain a live round (this always made him feel better when riding his machine. Because if he crashed. He did not want to also worry about the possibility of accidentally shooting himself on top of a severe case of road rash). He grabbed his helmet off of the edge of his desk and made his way wearily to the door of the station house. He was moving at the speed that would have made a Hollywood zombie feel like a cheetah. And when he finally reached the door the blast of chilled early-morning air was like a vitamin B shot for the soul, which only seemed to get stronger the closer he got to his machine because he knew that fooling his brain into thinking it was flying would help take the weight of an as yet unsolved murder off of his shoulders.

He placed his helmet on the back of his head to free his hands so that he could place them into his well broken in deer skin riding gloves secured the sternum strap on his go bag to ensure that it would not throw off his weight distribution when taking a corner. He swung his leg over the machine, and eased himself into the saddle as though he were climbing into a bubbling Jacuzzi. And in his mind he was even before he placed the key into the ignition. He could feel the stress of the day starting to melt away, he placed the key into the ignition and turned into the on position and he heard the familiar whine of the battery and other electronic components, warming up. He pressed the ignition switch and the dragon roared to life. Ian cracked the throttle a few times to bring up the RPMs and make sure the dragon was fully awake. When satisfied that he was ready, pressed his foot down on the gear lever, bringing the machine out of neutral and into first he waited at the edge of the parking lot for a split second, to be sure that there was no oncoming traffic, and then making a rather rapid ascent in the gearbox. He was in third gear in what seemed like microseconds.

As he wound his way down the highway decelerating through the corners with his knee getting very close to the payment, but not quite touching. You thought about everything, as he always did his best thinking on the machine. You thought about what Jenny might be doing if he still thought about him and wondered how he was doing. In his new position as a homicide detective or whether she had forgotten about him and moved on to someone else altogether, he also thought about the case and this avenging angel drug and other reasons besides, a monetary gain, or being blackmailed that someone would have for murdering Maggie Simmons he learned from his training officer. What seemed like an eternity ago that not discounting the odd drug-induced rampage. The three most common reasons for murder were most often, money, love and revenge. The last two, often working in tandem with one another, Rite was almost certain in Maggie's case. It wasn't money, because nothing of significant value other than the computer of course was missing from her apartment. And they had also run a check on her financials to see if she had made any significant monetary withdrawals or had received a significant sum of money that would've been out of character for a pharmaceutical research and development scientist. She had not and it wasn't revenge, because everyone today I talked to from her coworkers to her landlady had all said the same thing. And that was that everyone absolutely loved Maggie Simmons.

So, if it wasn't money or revenge, and if his training officers theory held any water that would just leave love as the supreme motivating factor. The problem was however that Maggie didn't have a boyfriend or husband or close family for that matter that would represent a prime suspect. There was something he was missing, and it was frustrating to Rite that he could not figure it out because the solution felt as though it were on the tip of his tongue or in the back of his brain somewhere. He just could not access the information. It kind of reminded him of this sensation that he sometimes got when waking up from a dream. Being able to see pieces of the dream, but not able to fully recall what the dream was about in its entirety and then having it slowly fade away.

As he made the last and most adrenaline pumping corner before the last straight mile that it would lead him to his driveway. He remembered something Sir Arthur Conan Doyle's famous detective Sherlock Holmes would often say which was something to the effect of "when you eliminate all probable possibilities whatever is left no matter how improbable, must be the answer" and as Rite dropped into first gear and semi-coasted into his garage. He thought to himself (it must have something to do with love, but what?). He dropped the shifter down into neutral, leaned the machine on its kickstand pressed the ignition switch into the off position and removed the key thus putting the dragon and Tiger back to sleep once more. He quietly thanked them both for bringing them home safe once again, and climbed off the machine.

Once inside, he repeated his ritual of placing his go bag and helmet on top of the old man's liquor cabinet and placing his piece in its drawer with an empty chamber in the magazine safely in its place on the pad and removed the bottle of Jamison and the highball glass from their sacred altar and poured himself. Three solid inches of the amber liquid, and then he ambled his way over to the docking station on the counter, where he kept his personal phone. There was a message from Jamie after the customary prompt to enter his password. A robotic voice told him "you have one new message" which was shortly followed by the sweet yet tired sound of Jenny's voice. "I just wanted to tell you that I love you and miss your face and wish you all the love in the universe." And with that small dose of love and happiness, the message was completed Rite let out a sigh of contentment and happily thought (well at least I'm still on the totem pole; I will have to call her this weekend, and check in). He placed the phone back into the cradle and strolled over to the stereo and inserted a CD of the re-mastered recording of "some kind of blue." By Miles Davis, and although he supposed this album was available in the form of MP3. He preferred to have it as a hard copy as files can be corrupted, but a CD is much harder to damage. Besides, it is impossible to feel an MP3 but a CD is something you can physically touch and see exactly where the music is coming from and that gave rite a strange sense of satisfaction that sense of satisfaction, as well as peace was dramatically amplified as the first notes (So What) came drifting out of the speakers. For some reason when he played Miles Davis, especially this album Rite felt as though he could see the music rather than hear or feel it. He could almost reach out and grab the notes out of the air, the music also seemed to stimulate his brain and allow him to see things in a new way. He turned up the volume slightly closed his eyes for a second and just let the sound wash over him, and then forgetting that the files were still in his go bag. He walked back over to the liquor cabinet and retrieved them. And then with his whiskey and the files tucked under his arm, he made his way to easy chair flopped into a semi-reclined position and opened Maxine Fillmore's file as though he were opening the Sunday morning newspaper for a leisurely read, he slowly sipped his whiskey while reading about her academic history college and the premed courses, and then law school. Nothing particularly interesting from a criminal standpoint a couple of citations for disorderly conduct during some sort of environmental protest but as far as Rite was concerned a disorderly conduct citation at a college protest is simply part of the process of finding oneself and he did demonstrate to Rite at least on a small level that Maxine Fillmore was willing to stand up for what she believed in. How far she was willing to go on the other hand, he was not sure.

After thoroughly reading about Maxine Fillmore, he decided that he should read about Brian some because of this point he didn't believe he was going to sleep anyway, and he had good train of thought going thanks to Miles. So why derail it, reading Brian's file was like getting a guided tour into the mind of a genius. He had the best grade point average, Rite had ever seen. He was solving math problems in his 20's that even some professors couldn't solve in their 40's and in his 30's he was already one of the top pharmaceutical research and development scientists in the country and in his 40's he became the youngest project manager in the history of White Light pharmaceuticals.

To Rite's surprise in the back of Brian Fillmore's White Light pharmaceutical dossier there was a copy of Brian Fillmore's medical records. Rite found it strange at first but then supposed it probably had something to do with the company's insurance policies as they wanted to make sure their employees, who would be handling the substances used to make up the formulas for a specific drug were not going to have an allergic reaction that may cause them severe bodily harm. Rite was skimming down the allergies and medical diagnosis list included in the dossier, when all of a sudden it hit him like a ton of bricks, and he bolted upright from the chair almost spitting out a mouthful of whiskey "holy Shiite. Jesus Christ on a stick!!! He has MS!!!!" This put everything in an entirely new light. His mind was moving faster than a Japanese bullet train out of Tokyo (it makes perfect sense that would explain why only the computer was missing and why Maggie's body was treated with such reverence. Either Brian or Maxine Fillmore, or maybe even one of the members of their team had killed Maggie Simmons. When she found out they were tampering with the results of the study. In order to push the drug to FDA qualifications, it wasn't because someone was being blackmailed or because they needed the money they needed the drug for Brian Fillmore. They needed the drugs to be proven to work successfully so that he could keep taking it and stave off the effects of his own medical problems. These thoughts were swirling around in his brain so fast he felt like he was caught in a Texas tornado. He grabbed for his work phone and pressed the number for speed dial so hard he thought his thumb would go to the phone. Summer's answered. "Rite? Do you know what fracking time it is?" "Of course I do. It's time for me to tell you that I've figured it out." What the hell are you talking about, figured what out?" Figured out why Maggie Simmons was murdered." Rite said, sounding more than a little triumphant. He could tell that Summers was definitely not sleeping anymore as the tone in her voice had switched from one of hostility and annoyance to one of joy and jubilation.

"Well stop beating around the bush and get to the point." Summers encouraged excitedly so he began to explain the theory he had developed concerning the fact that Brian Fillmore was dealing with multiple sclerosis himself and how Maxine Fillmore had become aware of Maggie's intentions to report to the drug developers and the FDA hell of ending Angel was not ready for human protocols, which would then of course mean that the development of the drug would be set back a considerable amount of time, and how Maxine Fillmore must've figured that the amount of time that it would take to reengineer the drug would mean that her husband's disease would have that much more time to progress and now he was betting that she figured the drug could be improved after it had passed. The FDA inspections would be afforded would be put into widespread use. Rite bet that Max rationalized it by telling herself that the really horrible side effects only affected a very small number of patients, and she needed the drug to work to help her husband.

Summers seemed to agree with Rite's for why Maggie was murdered and they both agreed that first thing in the morning they would pay a visit to Mr. and Mrs. Fillmore and rattle their cages and see how much of Rite's theory would stick, but Summers thought you should check in with Capt. Swift simply because legal pharmaceuticals with such a high profile company with very powerful supporters, it could turn into a public relations nightmare for the police department is not handled correctly Rite agreed with Summers that that if they were not careful their careers would definitely suffer. However, he was not so keen on involving Capt. Swift as he was never much of a by the book kind of guy and he dealing with the brass as they always seemed to be more interested in office politics and their reputations. Rather than actually bringing those that deserve it to justice nevertheless, they informed Capt. Swift of their intentions to pursue this line of questioning shortly after entering the precinct (which they both did relatively early as neither one could stop their mind from thinking about the case).

Chapter 9

They both stood in Capt. Swift's office at 8 in the morning explaining their theory on the murder of Maggie Simmons. When they had finished outlining it for her, she cleared her throat in a very authoritative manner and said "I will always go to bat for any one of my officers. As long as they have a sound theory and the evidence to back it up so the two of you better make sure that you have some solid evidence before we go picking a fight with one of the largest pharmaceutical companies in North America." Both Summers and Rite adamantly that we assured her that they would have a rock solid case before they poked the bear they let Capt. Swift's office and Rite picked up the phone to call Brian Fillmore and inform him that they had a few more questions that needed to be answered. And as before, Brian Fillmore assured them that he would be more than happy to help. Brian Fillmore asked them, when he and his wife would need to report to the station and Rite told him the afternoon would be fine and 1:30 PM would be all right. Brian Fillmore said that would be just fine and the next he would be there.

So for the rest of the morning Rite and Summers read and reread on Brian and Maxine Fillmore. To make sure that there was nothing that they had missed as well as working for any holes that the theory might have ended the more they read the more they were convinced that this was the only logical explanation, as they could not find anyone else on the drug development team or in the company that would directly benefit from the death of Maggie Simmons (after all possible outcomes have been exhausted. Whatever is left, no matter how improbable, must be the truth) ran through Rites head again and the new love could make people do very strange things indeed. He had seen it on many undercover operation women who are willing to lie and take the fall for the men in their life. Even if those men happen to be abusing them (love was a very powerful medicine indeed) Rite thought.

Both he and Summers agreed that they should make it clear that they knew that Max's father was a cop. And that they know about Brian Fillmore's current medical problems. Just to see what sort of response they would as people often slipped up (even lawyers). When they are caught off balance and having someone off balance was a good way to learn some new and useful information that might not otherwise be learnt.

Shortly after 1:30 PM, Mr. and Mrs. Fillmore arrived as promised, as Rite and Summers took them into the conference room that they had used for their previous conversation. Mr. Fillmore was dressed in usual geek chic business suit and greeted both the detectives warmly and asked about progress of the case and Rite assured him that they were getting closer to discovering exactly why Maggie Simmons had been murdered. Although there were a few questions that still remain unanswered. Unlike her husband, Maxine Fillmore seemed a little uneasy. Not necessarily nervous. More on edge than anything Rite assumed this was because as a lawyer she would have a pretty good idea that detectives only called you in after your initial interview when they had discovered a new piece of evidence or some new information that could be useful in solving the case, taking note of Maxine's edginess Rite said "I'm sure Mrs. Fillmore that you know that cops often have to interview people multiple times. Especially as new information is required for the case (she shot him a slight look as if to say. I know you're up to something). She nodded, unsure as a lawyer. You spent many hours going over and over the same questions in a different format in multiple interviews with your client. I'm also sure that your father probably complained about having to do the very same thing from the other side of the table when he was a police officer" at this revelation. Maxine's eyes widened slightly and she shifted fractionally in her chair. And this miniscule action gave Rite a sense of satisfaction that he was on the right track.

"How can we hope you today, detectives?" Brian Fillmore asked. "We just have a few questions about the process of getting a drug to market in the modern world. The drugs have to go through a stringent FDA inspection for side effects before they can be used by the general public. Do they not?" "Yes, Detective, that is correct. The FDA is very specific on their guidelines. Unfortunately, all drugs are going to have at least some slight negative side effects. The degree of which will vary significantly depending on the individual patient" "and what happens if a particular medication, cannot get a portion of side effects to fall within the FDA guideline?" "Well, then Detective, the drug will have to be reengineered until it does. And in some cases this may mean engineering the drug from scratch, which takes a considerable amount of time and effort not to mention a monetary loss for the company."

Rite interjected. "And while the drug is being reengineered, can it be used at all?" Maxine answered the question "that depends entirely on the severity of the side effects, typically no, the drug is not available. However in some cases, testing can still be done in small quantities, but the date of the release of the drug will be pushed back until it meets the FDA specifications" "I understand that as far as being available to the public is concerned. But what I am asking is whether or not he feels that the current formula under review can still be produced. While the formula is being reengineered" Detective Rite asked this time Brian reentered the conversation. "Yes, of course, we continue to produce small quantities of the drug under the current formula. We need them, so we can test each aspect of the medication so that we can bring it up to snuff with the guidelines." Detective Rite took some notes, and then said. "In essence, the medication is available in pill form in the lab for testing purposes so someone could get their hands on the medication and use it?" "Yes, I suppose so, Detective. But if the drug does not pass the inspection the first time, I do not know anyone that would risk taking a medication that could potentially kill them faster than the disease. They are suffering from, no matter how bad a condition they are in.

Detective Summers gave Brian a sympathetic look. "Are you sure about that Mr. Fillmore? Detective Rite and my-self know that you have MS and that is rapidly progressing." Brian Fillmore looked at them with an expression of slight surprise, but not to worry. "Well, I see you have thoroughly read my medical records that must have been included in my company file (Detective Summers nodded.) Yes it is true. I have MS, and yes it is progressing faster than I would like. But that does not mean I would risk taking a drug that has not been approved for use no matter how much promise it showed. Why would I do that, if I need to be around to assist in reengineering the drug so that we can help millions of people suffering from this disease, MS is a horrible disease. Eventually your body ceases to listen to you and you become trapped in your own head a living ghost, as it were, and that is not a life I would wish for anyone." So in a more direct answer to your question detective know I have never taken the drug in its current formula to lessen the effects of my own battle with MS." Detective Summers made some more notes, and then said. "We know that Maggie found out that the records of the clinical trial were being doctored to show more positive results without the side effects. And we know that she was going to blow the whistle with the help of reporter and you yourself told us that you had several discussions with Maggie about the fact that she felt that the medication was not ready to go to market and should not be approved for use until this problem was sorted out." Yes that is true Detective. We did have discussions about the fact that someone may have been tampering with the data of the clinical trials. But as I told you previously, I could find no evidence to support this fact. And you can't possibly be suggesting that I murdered Maggie to cover up the fact that the drug was unsafe. I love her like a daughter and would never do anything to hurt her. But if you're suggesting that someone did, then God help the individual"

That's good to hear Mr. Fillmore, because we checked. Maggie's phone again and found something very interesting. She had installed a GPS tracking device, which means that with access to a computer you can see everywhere she went over the past month, and we know after the last phone conversation she had with you she went to your house. We suppose to show you, physical evidence that the drug was not ready." Brian looked at both the detectives seriously. "The last conversation that I had with Maggie was on the morning of the day she died. And if she came by the house to show me evidence of the drug's weaknesses, I am not at all aware of it. I must've been on my way to the lab when she stopped by."

"Although you may have been out Mr. Fillmore, but we believe Maggie did meet someone at your house and tried to show them. The research on the drug and explained that she was going to tell the board and if that didn't work. She was going to tell a friend who worked for the Seattle Sun, because she knew that would definitely bring attention to the drug problems and make sure that no one else was hurt by its incomplete form." Brian Fillmore started to get angry. "You can be suggesting only one person met with Maggie, and that would be my wife, and by that suggestion you are inferring with Maggie's death. That is absolutely outrageous detectives, and I will not stand idly by while you slander the names of my family!! He said, severely irritated now. "It is a logical assumption sir as no one else but you and your wife live in your house. And according to the GPS program on the phone. Maggie was located at your residence for at least 20 minutes, and if she wanted to see you so urgently. There is no way she would've pounded on your door for 20 minutes with no answer, which indicates that Maggie talked to someone at your residence (Max began to squirm a little more obviously in the chair, which delighted Rite even more).

Rite looked directly at Maxine and somewhat forcefully said. "Did she try to tell you about the information that she had discovered in regards to avenging angels side effects? You argued about her blowing the whistle, and how important is that it was for the drug's development to stay on schedule, because your husband needed the drug to stave off symptoms, and it was important that he remain as healthy as possible for as long as he could because you knew that the drugs he could develop over the next few years, would save countless lives. Not to mention the fact that you truly love your husband and couldn't bear the thought of him suffering the effects of this disease." Maxine Fillmore started to look very uncomfortable indeed a few times. She acted like she was going to say something and then stopped Rite pressed her little more "all that Maggie told you about the disparities in the study. And that she was going to tell Brian about the problems with the drug. And you knew that that would be years of lost time in developing a better drug and then during the lost years your husband's symptoms would progressively get worse. And so you told her about Brian's illness hoping that that would convince her not to blow the whistle so that the drug would be approved by the FDA and your husband could then legally be treated by the drug without compromise or scandal. And when Maggie told you that it didn't matter, she was still going to show your husband the information anyway because he would want to know you just could not let that happen and you knew that if she couldn't find your husband she would eventually end up in the lab to double-check the information for herself as she was always a very studious individual so that would leave you plenty of time to let yourself into her apartment with his spare key that she is giving you in case of emergencies most likely. As we could not find any forced entry. So you waited until late. When she finally did return home, you try to reason with her one more time but when that didn't work. You gave her a shot of adrenaline that you had commandeered from the lab or some other source, possibly not intending to kill her, but only put her out of commission long enough to make it through the inspection process. I'll bet you figured that the adrenaline would look like a mild heart attack or embolism, and with the proper treatment. She would be just fine in a few months. However, when things went pear shaped, and she died. You used to stab wounds to hide the injection point of the needle and distract us from the cause of death. Figuring that with such obvious wounds, we would not be paying very close attention and would put the murder down to a robbery gone wrong is that about the size of it. Mrs. Fillmore?"

Maxine Fillmore started to say something. "I... I... I only wanted to... to help Brian the drug didn't pass inspection by the time it was fixed. His symptoms would have progressed too far for the drug to do any real good for him. And I would lose my husband, and even though there were side effects. I felt that it would be worth the risk and that he would be one of the ones that would come out all right. She just wouldn't listen, saying that Bryant wouldn't want to hurt anyone. Even if he was sick and could benefit from the drug. As you say detectives. I didn't want to hurt her. I thought the adrenaline would only make her ill for a very short period of time. And I used it because it would be untraceable is a natural substance produced by the body and would pass through the system, showing no anomalies in any sort of screening." And all of a sudden remembering that she was a lawyer suddenly said "I want my representation now."

As detective Summers slowly stood her up and placed her in handcuffs simultaneously advising her of her rights. While this was going on, Brian Fillmore looked absolutely mortified and kept repeating "it's not possible. She was like a daughter to us. She was one of the sweetest people on the planet. She would have never hurt anyone. If you would have let her show me the information we could have fixed it. It may take some time, but we could have fixed it and everything would've been fine. I can't believe you would do this." He kept shaking his head slowly, with tears streaming down his face.

Shortly thereafter, Maxine Fillmore's lawyer arrived and they had managed to establish that although it was murder in the first degree. It was not premeditated and was a crime of passion. Maxine Fillmore pleaded guilty to the crime and Rite and Summers both knew that she would receive no less than 15 years in the state correctional facility for women.
Simmons said she just couldn't get over how someone could murder. An individual they consider to be family, to preserve another family member's life. Rite just sort of shrugged and said, love makes people do very strange things that even they don't know they're capable until after they've done them.

After they've finished filling out the requisite amount of paperwork and booking. Mrs. Fillmore into custody, Rite and Summers decided to call it an early day as it was sunny and slightly warm and anyone that lives in Seattle knows it is necessary to take advantage of whatever Sun is available, because no one ever knew when exactly they would see it again, and as they both placed their final signatures on the form and headed for the station door, Summers looked at Rite and said "I think you'll make a decent homicide detective. I might keep you around for a while." He smiled and said I will take that as a compliment." And he gave her a wink, and at the bottom of the stairs they said their goodbyes and headed off in the direction of their vehicles and as Rite brought the Dragon to life he couldn't help but think of Jenni and wondered just how much a ticket to New York would cost this time of year. He released the clutch, dropped into first gear, merged into traffic and made his way home, where he would find a bottle of whiskey, and the voice of an angel.

The End.......or is it.

Links

Please leave a review at lulu or goodreads.

If you enjoyed this book, please view Hunted Heiress.
Available in Kindle format here, http://www.amazon.com/Hunted-Heiress-Aeriell-Lawton-ebook/dp/B00CELBCXW
Audio book version here, http://www.amazon.com/Hunted-Heiress/dp/B00E1P7I78.
iTunes, https://itunes.apple.com/us/book/hunted-heiress/id641300659?mt=11.
Paperback version, http://www.lulu.com/us/en/shop/aeriell-lawton/hunted-heiress/paperback/product-21053857.html
Hardback version, http://www.lulu.com/shop/aeriell-lawton/hunted-heiress/hardcover/product-21129887.html
ePub version, http://www.lulu.com/shop/aeriell-lawton/hunted-heiress/ebook/product-20987050.html

www.ingramcontent.com/pod-product-compliance
Lightning Source LLC
Chambersburg PA
CBHW050914120626
46552CB00004B/1574